Why
do people drink
Alcohol?

Julie Johnson

RAINTREE
STECK-VAUGHN
PUBLISHERS

RSVP

A Harcourt Company

Austin   New York
www.steck-vaughn.com

Published by Raintree Steck-Vaughn Publishers, an imprint of Steck-Vaughn Company

Library of Congress Cataloging-in-Publication Data
Johnson, Julie.
Why do people drink alcohol? / Julie Johnson.
    p.   cm.—(Exploring tough issues)
Includes bibliographical references and index.
ISBN 0-7398-3235-2
1. Alcoholism—Juvenile literature. 2. Drinking of alcoholic beverages—Juvenile literature.
[1. Alcohol. 2. Alcoholism. 3. Drinking of alcoholic beverages.] I. Title. II. Series.

HV5066 .J58 2001
362.292—dc21   00–062825

Printed in Italy. Bound in the United States.
1 2 3 4 5 6 7 8 9 0 05 04 03 02 01

Picture acknowledgments
The publisher would like to thank the following for their kind permission to use their pictures: Allsport 45; UK Bridgeman Art Library 12; Camera Press 22; Cephas *(title page)*, 8, 41; Mary Evans 10; Eye Ubiquitous/ Paul Seheult 42; Ronald Grant Archives 31; Angela Hampton 14, 38; Robert Harding 6 (bottom) 27, 30; Hodder Wayland Picture Library 11 (top and bottom), 13, 40/ A. Haslon 16 (bottom)/ Gordon Clements 17/ Tizzie Knowles 20, 37/ Howard J Davies 28; Impact/ Alex MacNaughton 4, 23/ Steve Parry 9/ Andy Johnstone 19, 25, 29, 44 / Bruce Stephens 36; Panos 18/ Liba Taylor 5, 24/ Sean Sprague 7/ Mark Schlossman 33/ Clive Shirley 35/ Giacomo Pirozzi 42; Popperfoto 26, 32, 39; Skyjold 16 (top); Tony Stone *(cover)*; Topham Picturepoint 34.

Contents

1. What is alcohol?   4

2. Alcohol—past and present   10

3. What does alcohol do?   18

4. Why do people drink
   alcohol?   26

5. What are the problems
   with alcohol?   32

6. Making choices
   about alcohol   40

Glossary   46

Further Information   47

Index   48

1. What is alcohol?

What do you think alcohol is?

Do you take drugs? If you asked most people this question, they would reply that they do not. However, if they take medicines, drink alcohol, smoke cigarettes, or even drink tea or coffee they are drug users. These are all drugs or substances that affect the mind and body in some way.

▲ Young women having a drink together after work—social drinking is part of life for many people.

A drug is something that when taken into our bodies changes the way our bodies work. Alcohol is a depressant drug because it causes our bodies to slow down as we lose our inhibitions. Sometimes alcohol makes people slur their words, but it can also make them more talkative.

FACT:
Alcohol is often not thought of as a drug—largely because its use is so common for both religious and social purposes in most parts of the world. It is a drug, however, and compulsive drinking in excess is one of modern society's most serious problems.
Addiction Research Foundation, Toronto, Canada

In most parts of the world, alcohol is a socially accepted drug. It is a legal drug, that is used by many people in lots of different places, for a variety of reasons. People may have a beer at a party, a glass of wine with a meal, or visit a bar on their way home from work. Some people use alcohol to help them relax at the end of a busy day. Homeless people may drink alcohol to help them cope with being jobless or homeless.

"I think that as long as you drink in moderation, alcohol is OK. It's when people go out and get drunk that the problems begin."
Sophia, 16

▼ *A group of Mexicans enjoy a beer together.*

How is alcohol made?

Alcohol is a chemical called ethyl alcohol, or ethanol. Alcohol can be made from most kinds of food, including fruits, grains, or vegetables. It is made through processes called fermentation and distillation. These processes produce an intoxicating drink that can vary in strength, depending on how it is made. Ethanol is a clear liquid, but different kinds of alcohol get their color from the products that are added during or after fermentation.

Beer is usually made from hops or barley mixed with water. Yeast is then added, and fermentation begins. The fermentation slowly produces alcohol.

▼ Spirits, such as whiskey, are distilled in large factories like this one in Scotland.

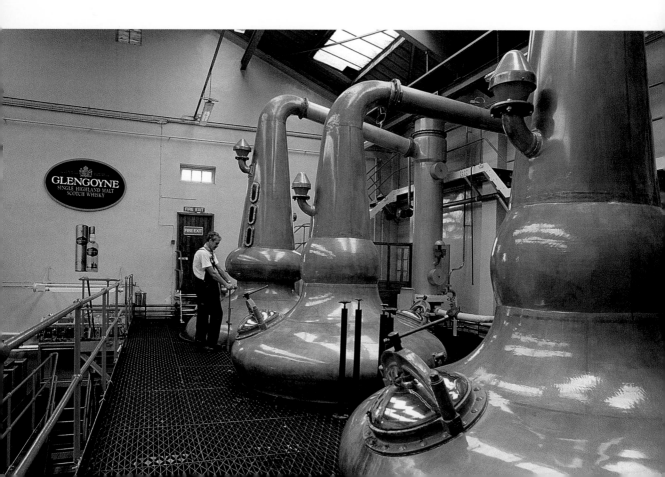

Wine can be made from many things, for example, fruits, rice, or vegetables such as potatoes and parsnips. The most widely drunk wine is made from grapes. The juice of the crushed grapes is mixed with yeast and left to ferment in a warm environment. Yeast gradually changes the sugar in the juice into alcohol.

Spirits (whisky, vodka, gin, and rum) are also made from grains, fruits, and vegetables. Whisky is made from malted barley. Vodka is made from wheat, rye, or potatoes. Gin is usually made from rye or barley and then flavored with juniper berries. Spirits are first fermented and then distilled to make the alcohol content stronger and purer. The spirit is then stored for between six months and several years to improve the taste.

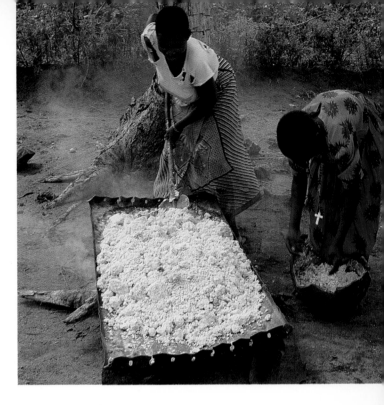

▲ *These women are making beer, using a local recipe, in Tanzania, Africa.*

FACT:
Many different countries have their own traditional drink made from local produce. In Ireland people drink poteen, a strong spirit made from potatoes. In Jamaica, there is a local gin made from bananas.

Types of alcohol

There are many kinds of alcohol made throughout the world. These vary from region to region depending upon the ingredients available in that area. The main types of alcohol are:

- beers (includes lager, ale, and stout)
- wines (includes white, rosé, and red wine, and sparkling wines such as champagne)
- ciders (from fruits such as apples or pears)
- fortified wine (includes sherry, port, and vermouth)
- spirits (includes whisky, gin, vodka, brandy, and rum)
- liqueurs or flavored spirits

Each type of alcoholic drink contains a different amount of pure alcohol. Beer and wine have less alcohol than spirits or fortified wine. For example, beer contains about 3.5 to 5 percent alcohol by volume, wine holds about 12 percent alcohol by volume, fortified wines contain about 20 percent alcohol by volume, and spirits usually contain about 40 percent or more alcohol by volume.

▼ *Different kinds of alcohol are lined up on a bar counter. Some drinks are drunk straight, while others have mixers added.*

Jake's first experience of strong alcohol came when he was on vacation when he was 14 years old. In the bars, the bar staff didn't ask people to prove how old they were, and Jake and his friends were able to get any type of drink they wanted. Jake usually drank beer, but he decided to try spirits for the first time. After an hour, he began to feel dizzy and sick. Later he threw up all over his friend. He felt awful the next day and had a terrible hangover —one he'll never forget.

Some alcohol, such as wine, is usually drunk by itself. Other types of alcohol can be either drunk on their own or mixed with another beverage. In Great Britain, some people add lemonade to beer to make shandy. Spirits are stronger than other forms of alcohol and are usually mixed with a nonalcoholic drink called a mixer. Mixers, such as lemonade, orange juice, tonic water, soda, or ginger ale are added to the spirit to make it taste better and not be as strong.

▶ *Many teenage boys try beer and experiment with spirits.*

2. Alcohol-past and present

Is alcohol something new?

People have been making and drinking alcohol for thousands of years. The earliest evidence of wine production dates back to nearly 6,000 years ago in the Middle East. The ancient Egyptians made beer from grain as early as 2250 B.C. In Scotland, pots containing traces of ale have been dated to about 2000 B.C. Some ancient peoples worshiped alcohol as a source of health and other benefits. The Romans had their own god of wine called Bacchus, and alcohol became an essential part of many Roman celebrations, social gatherings, and rituals.

▲ Bacchus, the god of wine, was worshiped by the Romans. Festivals in his honor were often drunken occasions.

FACT:
In the early twentieth century, small amounts of alcohol were sometimes used by mothers to calm restless babies. Up until the late twentieth century, mothers gave their babies gripe water, which contains alcohol. It was believed that gripe water would take away the discomfort of gas that babies often have after feeding.

▲ *Monks have produced and drunk alcohol throughout their history. This monk is drinking ale.*

There are references to alcohol in the Bible. After the great flood, Noah planted a vineyard and began to produce wine. However, he did not always restrain his drinking, and one day he got so drunk he collapsed.

Alcohol has been used through the centuries in a variety of ways. It has been used as a medicine for the seriously ill and has been given as a tonic for people who are run-down. For many years, wine was given to people to pep them up after a shock or illness. Spirits were even used as a painkiller before surgery. In Europe, it was often considered safer to drink ale rather than water, which carried many diseases.

▼ *This picture from 1823 shows people collecting and pressing apples to make cider.*

Alcohol abuse through the ages

Throughout history, the use and misuse of alcohol has been condemned. As more and more breweries and distilleries produced greater amounts of alcoholic drinks, drunkenness became an increasing problem.

In Elizabethan England (1558–1603), people who consumed too much alcohol were put into a bottomless beer barrel known as a "drunkard's cloak." Holes were cut in the side of the barrel for the offender's arms, and they were made to walk through the streets wearing the barrel.

▲ *This painting from the late eighteenth century shows the drunken behavior of men at a private club in London.*

By the eighteenth century, most countries had passed laws that attempted to regulate the use of alcohol. Licenses had to be granted to taverns and inns that wished to trade in alcohol. However, the consumption of alcohol steadily rose, as did concern about the misuse of alcohol.

The United States, Norway, Finland, Sweden, and Canada, all strongly Protestant countries, banned alcohol in the 1920s. The most famous of these campaigns against alcohol was started in 1920 in the United States and was called Prohibition. Prohibition aimed to stop the production and consumption of alcohol.

Despite more than 300,000 convictions for illegal drinking in this period, people continued to find ways to make and drink alcohol. Criminals, known as bootleggers, made money from the drinkers' illegal activities. Since there was no quality control on the alcohol being produced and sold, many people died from drinking impure alcohol. In 1933, the American public grew so unhappy with the situation that they insisted that Prohibition be stopped.

"Prohibition makes you want to cry into your beer and denies you the beer to cry into."
Don Marquis, archy and mehitabel, 1927.

◀ *During the American Prohibition era, people did strange things. This woman is wearing a special garment called a "Rummy Apron" in which she could hide her drink.*

The law and alcohol

Laws about drinking alcohol vary a great deal all over the world. There are laws about the age at which young people are allowed to use or buy alcohol. Other laws include where and when people can drink, and the measures of each kind of alcohol that can be sold on licensed premises.

> "Why do they make such strong drinks if they are dangerous? I think they should only let people at bars and pubs have a limited amount of alcohol."
> *Joanna, 12, Glasgow, Scotland*

In the United States, most states have raised the minimum legal age for drinking alcohol from 18 to 21. In New Zealand and Japan, the minimum age is 20. In Great Britain, the law gradually allows people more freedom to drink alcohol, and at 18, they are also allowed to buy alcohol from most licensed premises. In France, the laws governing alcohol are not as strict as in other countries—the minimum age for drinking is 14 to 18.

◀ *Despite the minimum legal age for drinking, underage drinking is an increasing problem in most countries.*

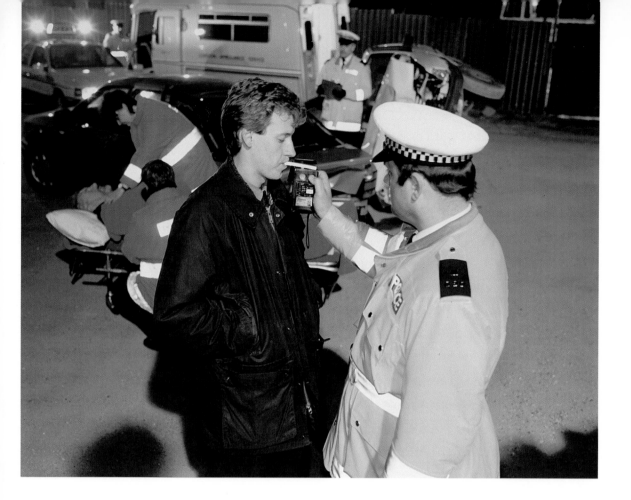

▲ A British policeman does a breathalyzer test on a driver who has been involved in a car accident.

Laws about alcohol, particularly about the minimum age for drinking, are often broken. In the United States, young people must present proof of their birth dates before they are allowed to purchase liquor. But it is too easy to ask an adult to buy alcoholic drinks for underage people, so the system is not foolproof.

The laws about drinking and driving also vary from country to country. Most countries have tried to crack down on drinking and driving with laws that aim to limit the amount people drink. Governments set a legal alcohol limit, and penalties for breaking these limits include heavy fines, disqualification from driving, and even prison sentences.

Religion and alcohol

Each religion has its own views on drinking alcohol. Most religions tolerate moderate drinking. However, some religions forbid any alcohol consumption.

Many Christians believe that it is acceptable to drink alcohol responsibly and in moderation. But some Christian groups, such as Baptists and Pentecostals, encourage their members not to drink at all. However, wine is used in some Christian religious ceremonies. Priests use wine in the Mass or Holy Communion service to represent the blood of Christ.

▲ *In many places, wine is part of the Christian Mass or Holy Communion service.*

In the Jewish faith, moderate and responsible use of alcohol is accepted. Wine is used in many Jewish religious ceremonies. One of these is Shabbat, the Sabbath observance celebrated every Friday night.

▲ *This Jewish family raises a glass of wine during Shabbat.*

At the beginning of the meal everyone eats a piece of bread while the father raises a glass of wine and blesses it, saying, "Blessed is the name of the Lord, King of the Universe, who has given us the fruit of the vine."
Then, everyone takes a sip of the wine.

In some Muslim countries, it is forbidden to drink alcohol or to have anything to do with people who produce and sell it. Strict Muslims are very careful not to come into any contact with alcohol. They should not even sell grapes to anyone who may make wine with them. To give or receive alcohol as a present is also forbidden. However, some Muslim countries, such as Turkey and Lebanon, do produce wine.

Sikhs believe it is important to remember God in everything they think and do. They are encouraged to keep a clear mind, so, for this reason, many Sikhs do not drink alcohol.

> "Keeping the body fit and healthy is part of serving God, for it is impossible to know and understand anything of the Creator's will if one is ill. Therefore a person should avoid anything whatever that undermines bodily health."
> *Maimonides (1135–1204), Jewish philosopher and Rabbinic scholar*

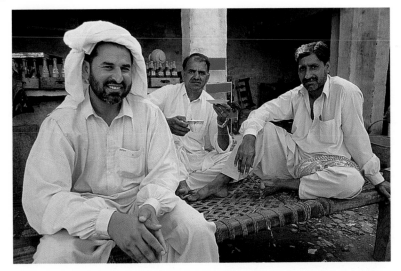

▶ *In Pakistan, Muslim men meet and socialize in teahouses where they enjoy drinking tea, rather than alcohol.*

3. What does alcohol do?

How does alcohol make you act and feel?

Alcohol goes first to the stomach and is then carried around the whole body and into each organ, including the brain, through the bloodstream. After one or two drinks, a person will begin to feel happy, relaxed, and carefree. As they continue to drink, they will begin to find it more difficult to do certain things, for example, to drive a car. The brain will no longer function properly, and it will become more difficult to remember things, to talk clearly, and even to walk properly.

If someone has had a lot to drink, people will say they are "drunk." If they continue drinking they will become very confused, collapse, and could even die from alcohol poisoning.

> "The first alcohol I tried was champagne at my aunt's wedding. I only had one glass and it made me feel all woozy."
> *Diana, age 13*

◀ *After one or two drinks, most people begin to feel more relaxed and carefree.*

▶ *Sometimes, after several drinks, people find themselves doing things they would never do normally—such as singing loudly and shouting.*

THE SHORT-TERM EFFECTS OF DRINKING ALCOHOL

Blood alcohol (mg/100ml)	Beer drunk (pints)	The effects on mind and body
20	$\frac{1}{2}$ - $\frac{3}{4}$	Judgment is affected, tension is released, feel more carefree.
50	$1\frac{1}{2}$	Tension and inhibitions of everyday life lessened. Driving performance affected.
60	2	Hand and arm movements affected, speech becomes clumsy. Driving affected badly.
80	$2\frac{1}{2}$ - 3	Begin to stagger, talk loudly, emotions are affected. Unsafe to drive.
100	3	Deeper areas of the brain affected, feel confused, may become sleepy.
160	5	May become aggressive. Memory loss is possible.
300	10	Difficult to arouse if asleep, not capable of voluntary action, equivalent to surgical anesthesia. Could lose control of bodily functions.
500	18	Coma, anesthesia of part of brain controlling breathing and heartbeat. Likely to die without medical assistance.

* This is a rough guide to the effects of drinking. Other factors, such as age, weight, and sex, determine an individual's reaction to alcohol.

What does alcohol do to your body?

Alcohol can cause long-term damage to the body if it is taken in large amounts regularly over months and years. However, young drinkers will not be damaged in the long term if they stop drinking or drink sensibly and follow guidelines for healthy drinking.

The whole of the body is affected by alcohol. These are the changes that happen to the main organs when a person drinks alcohol:

- heart—alcohol makes the heartbeat increase. This speeds up the rate that blood travels through the body. In the long term, this may cause problems with circulation and blood pressure.
- liver—the liver breaks down and eliminates alcohol and other toxins from the body. This process takes time, and the liver can only cope with 15 milligrams of alcohol every hour. This amount is nearly half a pint of beer or just less than one small glass of wine. In the long term, if someone drinks large amounts of alcohol every day, the liver works overtime and will eventually become damaged.

◀ *After a night of heavy drinking, you are likely to have a hangover the next day.*

These men are heavy drinkers. Many people who drink too much look older than they actually are.

- stomach—drinking too much alcohol in the long term can cause ulcers that are painful and can stop a person from being able to eat properly.
- brain—the brain is affected by alcohol very quickly. How the brain is affected will depend on how much alcohol a person has had to drink and how quickly the alcohol reaches the brain. If a meal is eaten while drinking alcohol, it takes longer for the alcohol to affect the brain. In the long term, drinking too much can cause sleeplessness, loss of memory, and anxiety.

FACT:
Pregnant women who drink risk having babies with fetal alcohol syndrome. The most serious defects include mental problems, growth deficiency, head and facial deformities, joint and limb abnormalities, and heart defects.
Facts About Alcohol, Addiction Research Foundation, Toronto, Canada

How much is it safe to drink?

Alcohol is measured in units. Each type of alcohol contains a certain number of units. For example, a standard glass of sherry contains one unit of alcohol. Half a pint of cider or a single shot of spirits also contain one unit.

Scientists are constantly studying how alcohol affects our health and how many units are safe for us to drink. Recent research found that small amounts, such as one to three units per day, of alcohol may protect a person against heart disease. Many people now drink some alcohol, especially red wine, each day for this reason. Other experts say that everyone should have at least one or two days each week that are alcohol-free.

But research can be misleading, and some health experts insist that drinking alcohol causes social problems that are just as dangerous to our health. Brawls after winning or losing a sports event and violence in that home can be triggered by excessive drinking. The important thing about drinking is knowing how much you can drink and knowing when to stop. Responsible drinking is all about knowing yourself and your own limitations.

▼ *Alcohol and violence often go together. This fight took place in May 2000 between Turkish and English soccer fans.*

case study · case study · case study

Paul had his eighteenth birthday party coming up. He wanted to celebrate with his friends but knew his mom and dad would be worried about alcohol and everyone getting too drunk. They were afraid that it would be like his older brother's party, when the neighbors called the police. Paul decided to talk it through with his parents and come to some kind of compromise. His parents had gone away for his brother's party, so they all decided it would be better if they were around for Paul's party. After talking it over, they planned a family party with a DJ for the young people. They decided there would be some alcohol but also lots of food and nonalcoholic drinks. Paul was really happy with how the party went. Everyone had a good time and nobody called the police.

▼ *Many young people don't think they can have a good time without alcohol.*

How does alcohol affect different people?

"My first experience of really drinking alcohol was when my uncle brought a crate of beer to a party. I had five or six bottles. I didn't really have too many problems, but I remember being very loud and people told me what embarrassing things I had said while drunk. I felt fine the next day. I think alcohol's an OK drug."

Paul, 15

"Mine was worse than that. Last summer on vacation we were at a party, and I got so drunk that I climbed up on the roof of a building. I lost my balance and ended up falling off—I really hurt myself. Then I was violently sick. I felt awful the next day. It's really put me off drinking. I don't think alcohol is an OK drug."

Marcus, 14

Alcohol is a very powerful drug, and it affects one person completely differently from another. The effects depend on several factors:

- how much alcohol has been drunk in a given period of time
- how the drink is taken—whether it's mixed with other kinds of alcohol or with mixers
- the drinker's sex
- the drinker's height and weight
- how much food is in the stomach
- what kind of mood the person is in already

▼ *This man is used to drinking his alcohol straight. Most people would become very drunk if they tried to drink like this.*

- previous experience of drinking—how used to alcohol a person is already. People who drink regularly become used to the side effects and can drink more before they suffer these bad effects
- current state of health

General guidelines for sensible drinking suggest that women should not drink more than 21 units of alcohol per week and that men should not drink more than 28 units of alcohol per week. Young people, who usually weigh less and are not as used to alcohol as most adults, should drink fewer units than the above guidelines for men and women.

▼ *Physically, women are less able to deal with alcohol, so the effects can be greater.*

4. Why do people drink alcohol?

The reasons people drink alcohol

People drink alcohol for many reasons but mostly because drinking helps them to enjoy themselves. It also helps people relax and to feel less shy. Many people think that the positive effects of drinking outweigh the negative effects.

"When I want to celebrate something really important, such as a birthday, I like champagne. At home, after work, I might have a glass of wine because I like the taste and because they say it's good for you!"
Lee, 27

▼ *World Champion Mika Hakkinen of Finland celebrates with champagne after the Spanish Formula One auto race in May 2000.*

Other reasons people drink alcohol include:

- to relax and relieve stress after a busy day
- to help people feel at ease when meeting new people
- to be sociable—many people feel alcohol is necessary at a party to make sure everyone has a good time
- to celebrate anything from a wedding, a christening, or a birthday, to winning a game
- to complement food and cooking—as well as adding flavor to food, people like to drink alcohol with their meals. In some countries, such as France and Italy, it is traditional to drink wine with most meals
- for health reasons—medical research shows that some alcohol can be good for you
- it's easily available. In many countries alcohol is sold in more and more outlets, such as supermarkets and convenience stores.
- out of habit—alcohol can be addictive
- peer influence

Young people and alcohol

Alcohol is a legal drug that is used by many young people. It is easily available to underage drinkers, because many of them look older than they really are and they can buy it from many liquor stores. Most people also keep some alcohol at home, and this is where the majority of young people first experience alcohol. In this situation, either their parents give the alcohol to them or they experiment with it secretly.

Other reasons young people decide to drink include:
- to get the buzz—alcohol can be exciting and fun
- to fit in with the crowd—peer influence
- to feel popular and less nervous in social situations
- to help to forget problems at home or school
- out of boredom—drinking alcohol is something to do on the weekends
- drinking seems more exciting and grown-up than other social activities such as sports or going to a movie

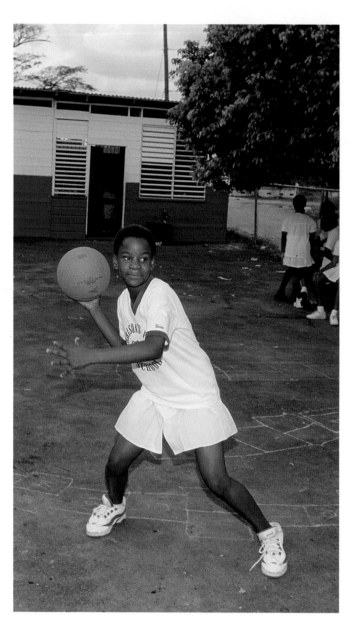

▲ *Playing sports for some young people is a good way to keep fit and avoid the habit of drinking too much alcohol.*

One of the main reasons young people drink is because they think it shows they are grown up. Boys may feel it makes them seem more like men. They think that drinking shows they are adults, while drinking large quantities and not getting drunk is macho. Girls may drink to show they can keep up with the boys. Research in many countries shows that young people are drinking earlier and drinking more.

FACT:
A new study shows that binge drinking on college campuses increased by 14% between 1993 and 1999. Binge drinking is defined as a man consuming five or more drinks in a row, or a woman having four or more consecutive drinks.
Journal of American College Health, 2000

▼ *These French students have had a lot to drink. Some young people are tempted to drink too much because their friends are doing the same.*

Why do advertising and the media make people drink?

▲ *Pictures and images used in advertising often show only the glamorous side of drinking alcohol.*

Even though alcohol is a drug, it is, for most people, socially acceptable. As a result, alcohol regularly appears in the media. Movies and television programs frequently show people drinking alcohol and having fun. And, during the commercial breaks, ads show similar exciting images.

FACT:
Research on responses to alcohol advertising on television showed that the more boys aged fourteen to seventeen liked the advertisements, the more likely they were to be drinkers, to have higher annual consumption (about 67 cans over the past year), and to expect to drink more frequently in the future.
Linda Hill, Young People and Alcohol, Child to Adult: The Dunedin Study

case study · case study · case study · case study · case study

Paul always watched a lot of movies and television. He particularly liked action films, and there were always cool people drinking beer. "It was always in my face; I just couldn't get away from it," he said. Paul was eleven when he decided to try beer with a group of school friends. One night, when Paul's parents were out, they found a case of beer in the garage and decided to drink it for a laugh. It was really good fun to start with—the beer didn't taste very nice but it made everyone giggle. They drank more and more and enjoyed dancing and messing around. Paul suddenly felt woozy. He threw up on the carpet and passed out. The next morning he felt terrible and told himself he'd never drink again.

Some people argue that alcohol is as bad for people's health as cigarettes. However, tobacco advertising is banned, while advertisements for alcohol are everywhere—on the television, in magazines, and on billboards. Advertisers of alcohol know that most people think drinking alcohol is sophisticated and fun. They play upon this fact by producing advertisements that show attractive people enjoying alcohol in exotic locations or in exciting situations. Some advertisements are specially targeted at younger people.

▶ *Some movies seem to glamorize drinking alcohol. In the movie* Cocktail, *Tom Cruise plays a hip young bartender.*

5. What are the problems with alcohol?

How does alcohol affect society?

Most people do not have problems with alcohol. However, as the number of people who drink rises, the problems associated with alcohol increase as well.

Drinking and driving is one of the most serious alcohol-related problems. Young drivers who drink are five times more likely to have an accident than non-drinkers. Many parents are concerned about the levels of drinking and driving among adults, as well as among young people. In the United States, a California mother, whose 13-year-old daughter was killed by a drunken driver in 1980, started the organization called MADD (Mothers Against Drunk Driving). The organization campaigns for stricter laws against drinking and driving and has 3 million members in the United States.

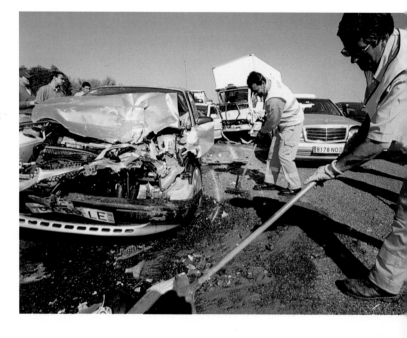

▶ The risk of a car accident is higher when the driver has been drinking.

An anti-drinking sign painted by children in Sri Lanka is a sad reminder of the problems with alcohol.

Every year, all over the world, many workdays are lost due to people being off sick with hangovers or other alcohol-related problems. This results in a loss of profit to many businesses.

The cost to hospitals and health services for alcohol-related illnesses is also increasing. Alcohol not only causes physical health problems, but it also contributes to mental health problems, such as depression and suicide.

There is also a growing number of crimes that are directly related to the use and abuse of alcohol. Violent crimes—especially domestic violence and child abuse—while under the influence of alcohol is on the increase.

"The majority of our patients come in with problems that are related to alcohol in some way or another. You have fights, car crashes, and accidents and then there is the illness, all of which are caused by too much alcohol over many years. Personally, I feel it is a very dangerous drug in every way."
Nurse in a large American city

33

What is alcohol dependency?

It is important to remember that alcohol is a drug and, as with any other drugs, one of the dangers is dependency or addiction. Some people become physically dependent on alcohol. This means that their bodies do not work properly without drinking and they feel sick if they do not have alcohol.

FACT:
Many famous people have been alcohol-dependent or had parents who were dependent on alcohol. Ludwig van Beethoven (1770-1827), the famous German composer, had an alcoholic father. As a result, Beethoven had to go out to work at an early age. He managed to support his family as a singer in the court chapel. Elvis Presley (1935-1977), the singer and actor, was just 42 when he died of what is thought to have been a combination of drug and alcohol abuse.

◄ Elvis Presley in 1971, just six years before he died. At the height of his success, Elvis had been a sex symbol, but here he is starting to look ill from years of alcohol and drug abuse.

Many people can drink alcohol in moderation, but others cannot control the amount they drink and alcohol begins to take over their lives. They don't drink for pleasure; they drink because they cannot do without alcohol.

We sometimes assume that people who are dependent on alcohol are loners or homeless. But many drinkers have good jobs with a home and a family to support. These people find it difficult to admit they have a problem with alcohol. They may not seem to get particularly drunk when they drink, but they need to drink to cope with their lives.

▼ *Alcohol dependency can mean drinking anything with alcohol in it. These South Africans drink a deadly mixture of beer and car battery fluid.*

How do people become alcohol-dependent?

There are many different reasons why someone becomes alcohol-dependent. It is not easy to say exactly why one person becomes alcohol-dependent and another does not. Some people do not cope well with stress and may have a particularly difficult home or work life. Perhaps something has happened in a person's life to make him or her depressed or lonely. Or the person may be poor or have a personality problem. Some people start drinking out of boredom but then drink out of habit and use drinking to cope with life.

FACT:
Those children who had tried alcohol by age nine were more likely than others to have experienced alcohol-related problems by age eighteen.
Linda Hill, Young People and Alcohol

◀ *Losing a husband or wife can be one of the many reasons somebody starts to drink heavily.*

case study · case study · case study · case study · case study

Sarah was a friend of Gail's for many years. Gail had noticed at times that Sarah's behavior was strange, secretive, and, once or twice, she had even lied about certain things. Gail never for one minute thought that Sarah was an alcoholic. Sarah was a nurse and held a very responsible position in the hospital where she worked. She was a kind and thoughtful person, and her patients thought the world of her. Then, one day, Sarah admitted herself to a special unit for treating people with alcohol problems. She told Gail she had been drinking heavily since she was 14 years old.

A person does not become alcohol-dependent overnight. It usually takes several years for alcohol dependency to develop. Some people drink heavily for many years without actually realizing that they are dependent on alcohol.

With the increasing number of teenagers starting to drink at a younger and younger age, governments around the world are concerned that there will be a rise in the number of young people who are dependent on alcohol over the next few years.

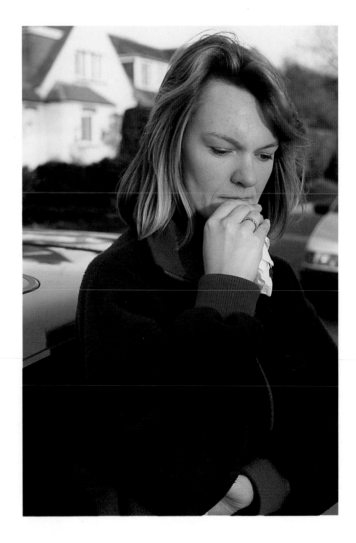

▶ *When the pressures of work and family life get too great, alcohol can seem the answer for some people.*

Where can people with drinking problems get help?

The most important first step for people with alcohol dependency is for them to admit that they have a problem and that they need help. Even then the road to recovery will not be easy, but unless they acknowledge that they have a problem with alcohol, they cannot start to get better.

Treatment for people with alcohol problems can be in hospitals or special units or at support meetings and counseling groups. The process of giving up alcohol or "drying out" is a long and difficult one. The person may need to receive medication to help deal with the painful withdrawal symptoms. They might need treatment for other conditions, such as liver or stomach problems, caused by years of heavy drinking.

▼ *Counseling is an important part of recovering from alcohol dependency.*

"I drank just to get rid of my feeling of not being wanted or really loved. It took me a broken marriage and nearly losing my job before I would admit that I needed help."
Shaun, aged 40, who started drinking at the age of 12

Many people who are dependent on alcohol need to learn to live without drinking ever again—this is called living in sobriety. Some people continue to drink in moderation, but this is difficult because they have an addiction. Many recovering dependent drinkers join an organization called Alcoholics Anonymous (AA). The organization provides people with the help and support of other recovering drinkers or ex-drinkers.

There are other organizations that can provide help for the families of dependent drinkers. These groups help the families support the recovering dependent drinker.

Many believe that once people are dependent on alcohol they are dependent for life. It is not easy to recover from being a dependent drinker, but many people, with the help of organizations like the AA, can overcome their dependency.

▶ *Help can be just a phone call away, but admitting there is a problem has to come first.*

6. Making choices about alcohol

What do different people think about alcohol?

▼ Drinking alcohol isn't always fun—this girl has just been sick and needs her friend's help.

People have many different thoughts and feelings about alcohol. Their opinions depend on their own personal experiences. Perhaps someone has an alcoholic in the family and he or she has seen the damage that alcohol can do to the whole family. If someone works as a nurse or ambulance driver, they see sick and injured people every day whose problems are caused by alcohol.

A young person who gets drunk for the first time and has fun might think drinking alcohol is exciting. A young person who gets drunk for the first time and is sick would probably have a very different opinion.

Everyone has their own thoughts about drinking alcohol. Listen to these different voices:

"A lot of the time with our work, alcohol has been involved in some way or another. I drink, but having seen all the problems that are caused by alcohol, I drink in moderation."

Ambulance driver, New York City

"Friday and Saturday night fights are triggered by people just not knowing when to stop drinking. This leads to arguments that end up in a big fight. This isn't just in the pubs and clubs but also in people's homes."

Policeman, Birmingham, England

"It's OK if you drink a little bit of alcohol and become merry. But if you drink a lot and become drunk it is not very nice for the people around you."

Julian, 13, Lille, France

"Come off it! A party with no booze? You must be joking."

Michael, 21, Manchester, England

"I like my glass of wine after a long day at work."

Janette, 31, Illinois

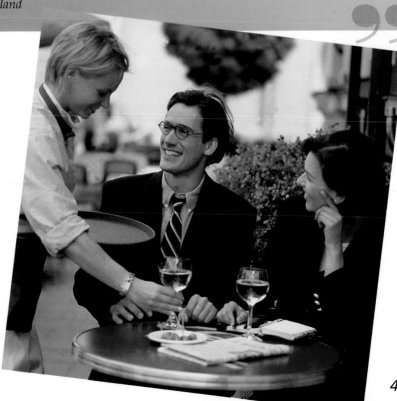

▶ *Many people can enjoy a drink without becoming alcoholics.*

Making choices about alcohol

Alcohol use among young people is rising. As we have seen, young people's ability to manage alcohol is not as effective as that of adults, but it can be done.

You all have choices to make when it comes to alcohol:

- you decide whether you want to drink or not
- you are in control of the amount you drink
- you can encourage your friends to drink or you can respect their choices
- you know when you're over the limit and can say "no" at any time

▲ *If you do drink alcohol, then only you can decide how much is right for you to drink.*

case study · case study · case study · case study · case study

When Kathy was 15 she saw alcohol as a rite of passage to growing up. If she could show everyone how much she could drink and that she could handle her alcohol then her friends would look up to her. One day she made a bet with Jo, her best friend. They bet on who could drink more. That was when it all went horribly wrong. They started drinking some beer and then, when it ran out, they stole vodka from Kathy's parents' liquor cabinet. Both girls drank until they passed out. Fortunately, Kathy's mother found them and called an ambulance. They both ended up in the hospital with alcohol poisoning.

FACT:
A survey of young people aged fifteen to sixteen found that many young people experience problems due to the misuse of alcohol. On average, 21% of teenagers reported individual problems, such as reduced performance at school. Some 22% reported relationship problems, 15% reported sexual problems, such as unwanted or unprotected sex, and 12% reported delinquency problems, such as violence and fighting.
1995 ESPAD Report, CAN and Council of Europe, 1997

Remember:
- 1 glass of wine   =   1 unit
- $1/2$ pint of beer/lager   =   1 unit
- 1 can of strong beer   =   3 units
- $1/2$ bottle of vodka   =   15 units
- 1 glass of a soft drink =   0 units

What choices will you make when it comes to alcohol?

▼ *After working all week, these young Zambian men enjoy a few beers on a Friday night—it's their way of relaxing.*

Being careful with alcohol

Alcohol is part of our society. Even though it is a dangerous drug and causes many problems in society, it is still legal. But it is possible to drink sensibly and carefully and have a good time.

Tips for sensible drinking:

- always have food with alcohol—alcohol drunk on an empty stomach is absorbed quickly into the body
- alternate nonalcoholic drinks with alcoholic drinks
- think about what you are drinking—generally the higher the alcohol content of the drink, the more quickly it is absorbed into your body. Vodka, for example, is absorbed faster than beer.
- do not mix your drinks—for example, wine and spirits shouldn't be mixed
- beware of spirits mixed with a soft drink—vodka and lemonade might not taste as strong as straight vodka, but it still has lots of alcohol in it
- try to drink only on weekends or on special occasions
- plan how much you are going to drink before you go out with your friends and stick to your plan

▼ *Drinking orange juice between each alcoholic drink is this girl's way of taking care she doesn't get too drunk—what would you do?*

- if someone says they do not want another drink, do not pressure them into having one
- if someone tries to pressure you into having another drink, and you don't want another, say "No!"—You are your own person, and you can stand up for yourself.

Alcohol is part of our society, and it is here to stay. It can be used safely, and in a fun way, without harming your health— it's up to you.

▲ *Drinking alcohol is just one way of having fun. Lots of young people find other things that give them a buzz.*

"One thing I know about alcohol is that it can be very dangerous and that it is not good to drink too much of it. You can become addicted to it and it can make you do things you do not want to do and it can influence your mind. It is OK to have a little bit of alcohol but not too much."
Katy, 11

GLOSSARY

Addiction
A person's inability to stop doing something, even when it is harmful.

Alcoholic
A person addicted to drinking alcohol.

Binge drinking
Drinking one alcoholic drink after another, very quickly.

Breweries
Buildings where beer or lager is produced.

Consumption
The purchase and use of something, e.g., alcohol.

Delinquency
Minor crimes, usually committed by young people.

Dependency
A person's need to have something to help them cope with life.

Depressant drug
A drug that causes the body to slow down. Alcohol is a depressant drug.

Distillation
The process of evaporating or boiling a liquid to make it more concentrated or purer.

Domestic violence
Physical abuse among family members, people who are married or are living together.

Drying out
An alcoholic's efforts to stop drinking.

Fermentation
A chemical reaction in which yeast breaks down the sugar in fruit, for example, and changes it to alcohol.

Growth deficiency
Development problem in a baby or child. Can begin as a baby is forming in the mother's womb.

Hangover
The aftereffects of drinking too much alcohol. Effects include headache, tiredness, and sickness.

Intoxicating
Something, such as alcohol, that makes a person drunk or over-excited.

Legal
Allowed by law.

License
Permission from an authority to allow bars, restaurants, liquor stores, etc., to sell alcohol.

Licensed premises
A place where alcohol may be sold.

Long term
Something that goes on for a long time.

Macho
Behavior that makes one look tough and cool. Usually used to describe boys and men.

Measure
A certain quantity or amount of a substance.

Minimum legal age
The youngest age at which people are allowed to do something by law.

Moderate drinking
Drinking amounts of alcohol that do not exceed the recommended weekly amounts.

Peer influence
Pressured to do something because everyone else is doing it.

Prohibit
To stop something from happening.

Short term
Something that happens for a short time.

Sober
In control and not drunk.

Sobriety
State of not being drunk from alcohol. We often say that a person lives in sobriety.

Teetotaler
A person who does not drink any alcohol.

Underage drinking
Drinking alcohol below the legal age for drinking.

FURTHER INFORMATION

ORGANIZATIONS

Worldwide there are organizations providing information and advice about alcohol. The organizations below can supply educational material and resources. Information is also available on the Internet.

Alcohol and Drug Problems Association of North America
1101 15th Street, NW
Suite 204
Washington, DC 20005

Alcoholics Anonymous
PO Box 459
Grand Central Station
New York, 10163
Tel: (212) 870 3400

MADD
(Mothers Against Drunk Driving)
511 E. John Carpenter Freeway
Irving, TX 75062

NCADD (National Council on Alcoholism and Drug Dependence)
12 West 21 Street
New York 10010
Tel: (212) 206 6770
http://www.ncadd.org

FURTHER READING

Clayton, Lawrence. *Alcohol Drug Dangers*. Enslow, 1999.

Haughton, Emma. *Alcohol*. Raintree Steck-Vaughn, 1999.

Kozar, Richard. *How to Get Help*. Chelsea House, 2000.

McGuire, Paula. *Alcohol*. Raintree Steck-Vaughn, 1998.

Peacock, Nancy. *Alcohol*. Chelsea House, 2000.

Pringle, Laurence. *Drinking: A Risky Business*. William Morrow, 1997.

Sanders, Pete, and Steve Myers. *Drinking Alcohol*. Copper Beech Books, 1997.

INDEX

Numbers in **bold** refer to pictures.

advertising 30, **30,** 31, **31**
alcohol
    benefits of 22, 27
    effects on the body 4, 18, **18,** 19, **19,** 20, **20,** 21, 24, 33
    effects on society 22, 32, 33, 44
    how it's made 6, **6,** 7, **7, 11**
    types of 8, **8**
    units 22, 25, 43
alcohol abuse 12, 13
alcohol dependency 27, 34 35, **35,** 36, 37, 38, 39
Alcoholics Anonymous 39

Bacchus 10, **10**
bars **8,** 9, 14, **31**
beer 5, **5,** 6, **7,** 8, 9, **9,** 10, 19, 24, 43, 44
binge drinking 29
breathalyzer test 15, **15**

car accidents **15,** 32, **32,** 33
cider 8, **11,** 22
counseling 38, **38**
crime 33

distillation 6, **6,** 7
domestic violence 33
drinking and driving 15, **15,** 19, 32, **32**

drugs 4, 5, 24, 28, 44
"drunkard's cloak" 12
drunkenness 5, 12, **12,** 18, **18,** 24, 31, 35

ethanol 6

fermentation 6, 7
France 14

gin 7, 8
grapes 7
guidelines for sensible drinking 25, 44, **44,** 45

hangovers 9, **20,** 33
health problems 38
history of alcohol 10, **10,** 11, **11,** 12, **12,** 13, **13**
homelessness 5

lager 8, 9
law and alcohol 13, 14, 15
Lebanon 17
licenses for alcohol 13, 14
liqueurs 8

media and alcohol 30, **30,** 31, **31**
Mexico **5**
mixers 8, 9, 24

New Zealand 14

parties 5, 23, 24, 27, **27**
peer influence 27, 28, **29,** 45

Presley, Elvis 34, **34**
problem drinking 34, **34,** 35, **35**
Prohibition 13, **13**
pubs 14

reasons for alcohol dependency 36, **36,** 37, **37**
reasons for drinking 5, 26, **26,** 27, **27,** 28, 29, **29**
religion and alcohol 4, 16, **16,** 17, **17**

spirits 7, 8, 9, 11, 22, 44

taverns 13
Turkey 17

underage drinking **14,** 15
UK 12, 14
United States 13, 14

violence and drinking 22, **22,** 33, 43
vodka 7, 8, 42, 44

whiskey 7, 8
wine 5, 7, 8, 9, 11, 16, **16,** 17, 22, 27, 44

young people and alcohol 9, **9, 19,** 23, **23,** 25, 28, 29, **29,** 30, 31, 37, 40, **40,** 41, 42, **42,** 43, **43**

48